D1171373

BALL
HOG

by HOSS MASTERSON   illustrated by JOSH ALVES

STONE ARCH BOOKS
a capstone imprint

is published by Stone Arch Books,
A Capstone Imprint
1710 Roe Crest Drive
North Mankato, Minnesota 56003
www.mycapstone.com

Cataloging in Publication information is available at the Library of Congress website.

ISBN: 978-1-4965-4308-0 (hardcover)
ISBN: 978-1-4965-4312-7 (paperback)
ISBN: 978-1-4965-4324-0 (eBook PDF)

Summary: Spikelle Jordan is a skilled basketball player for the Hedgehogs but needs
to learn to share the ball.

Illustrator: Josh Alves
Editor: Nate LeBoutillier
Designer: Kristi Carlson

Printed and bound in the USA.
010008S17

TABLE OF CONTENTS

HEDGEHOGS

11

GUARD

SPIKELLE JORDAN

MVPS

SPIKELLE JORDAN
This hedgehog has the best
b-ball skills around but
needs to learn to share.

MADDY MOONRAT
Spikelle's talented
teammate wants to
see Spikelle pass it.

COACH FURBALL
The Hedgehog coach is
nice but a bit nervous.

CHAPTER ONE

YOU TAKE IT OUT

The timeout ended, and the Hedgehogs broke their huddle. The fans began to cheer. The Hedgehogs were about to inbound the basketball.

The giant score clock that hung high up on the gym wall showed many numbers. It showed that the Hedgehogs had 44 points. It showed that the Ferrets had 45. It showed that only three seconds remained in the game.

There would be time for one pass. Maybe time for one dribble and one shot. No more. One last chance for a Hedgehog victory.

Maddy Moonrat and Spikelle Jordan walked to the sideline. They were the two Hedgehog guards and the team's best players. The referee stood with the ball, waiting for the timeout to end.

The Hedgette cheerleaders did their famous cheer. Three of them curled up into balls. The other three rolled them up and down the sideline, singing, "Roll on, Mighty Hogs, roll on!"

The Ferret fans tried to drown the cheers. But the Hedgie band was in full force. Drums banged, and horns rang out. The whole gym shook.

The Ferret fans shouted and stomped.

"**DE·FENSE!**" *Stomp stomp.*

"**DE·FENSE!**" *Stomp stomp.*

The Hedgehogs fans chanted and clapped. "**LET'S GO, HEDGIES!**" *Clap clap. Clap clap clap.*

The referee said, "Okay, here we go." He held the ball out to Spikelle.

Spikelle pulled her paws back.

So the referee turned to Maddy and held the ball out to her.

Maddy didn't want it. She turned her back.

The referee raised his eyebrows.

Spikelle thought of herself as the best shooter on the team. If Spikelle were the one to pass the ball in, she knew she would not get it back in time to make the last shot.

"You take it out," Spikelle told Maddy.

"No way," said Maddy, shaking her head. "You take it out, Spikelle."

"No," said Spikelle. "Take it out, Maddy."

"No," said Maddy to Spikelle. "You do it."

The referee held the ball out in front of him. "Someone needs to take this ball," he said.

Spikelle and Maddy stared at each other. Spikelle folded her arms. Maddy put her paws on her hips. Spikelle straightened her headband. Maddy rubbed her snout. Neither blinked.

Coach Furball waved his arms from the Hedgehog bench. "What are you waiting for?" he shouted.

The referee put the ball on the floor and said, "I'm counting to five. If nobody takes the ball and passes it in, it goes back to the Ferrets."

Spikelle and Maddy looked at the referee. The referee looked back at them.

"Are you counting to five out loud or in your head?" asked Maddy.

"In my head," said the referee.

"What are you at?" said Maddy.

"Three," said the referee.

"Oh, grubs and worms!" said Maddy. She grabbed the basketball off the floor. She slapped it and passed it to Spikelle.

Two Ferret players guarded Spikelle. It was impossible for Spikelle to see.

The three seconds on the score clock changed to two . . . then to one . . .

Spikelle danced free with a fancy dribble. She took a wild shot from way out. With the ball in the air, the final horn sounded.

Everyone's eyes followed the ball. The ball seemed to float in slow motion. Spikelle was the only one not watching. She knew what would happen. She turned away.

The basketball missed everything. Even the backboard.

The Ferrets began to dance. Their fans gave a mighty yell.

The Hedgehogs crowd hissed from the bleachers. They felt that their team should have won by 20 points. Instead, they had lost.

Someone in the stands yelled out, "What was number eleven *doing*?"

Another fan said, "Where's the coaching?"

Somebody else shouted, "The one with the spiky hair is more *ball* hog than hedgehog!"

"Yeah," said another fan. "That's for sure."

The Hedgehog crowd shuffled out of the gym. They muttered and complained all the way back to their hedgerows and hedge-homes.

CHAPTER TWO

BALL HOG

Coach Furball gathered his team in the locker room after the game. The players lined up on the bench. They sat with their heads down. They looked like a row of black and brown bowling balls.

"What happened out there?" asked Coach.

"Spikelle and Maddy were arguing," said one of the players. "Both of them wanted to take the last shot. But there was only one shot to take."

"I thought Coach wanted me to take the shot," said Spikelle.

"No," said Maddy. "You were supposed to pass the ball inbounds to me, Spikelle."

"That's not what I remember," said Spikelle.

"Well, didn't you tell Spikelle to take it out in the huddle?" Maddy asked Coach.

Coach Furball looked at his feet. He scratched an invisible itch. "Golly," he said. "I can't remember. I get a little nervous at the end of games."

Some of the players rolled their eyes.

Maddy stood. "That's not the real problem, anyway," she said.

"What do you mean?" said Coach Furball.

"It's like the fans were saying," Maddy said. "Spikelle is more *ball* hog than hedgehog."

"Yeah," said another teammate. "She wants to be the big shot hero. She wants all the glory."

Spikelle's eyes filled with tears.

"Spikelle wants to win just like the rest of you," Coach said.

Roxy Roller was the team's center. She was twice as big as the other hedgehogs. But she was also twice as shy. So it surprised the other players when she spoke up. "Coach," said Roxy, "Spikelle's amazing. No question. But I can't remember the last time she passed to me."

Other players spoke up. Those who didn't speak nodded their heads.

This hurt Spikelle's feelings. She put more time in on the court than any other hedgehog around. She worked hard to perfect her skills. Layups, jump shots, free throws. Both right paw and left. She had spent two hours that week working on her Super Spin dribble alone! Maddy practiced some, too. But the rest of her teammates — they were a little lazy.

Spikelle thought she deserved to take the last shot. She passed when she had to. But the last shot? For a chance to win the game? Come on. There's no way she wasn't taking that shot.

Coach Furball mopped his face with a towel. "Well," he said. "This *is* a team game. Maybe we got a little bit selfish out there at the end."

Coach Furball righted his crooked glasses on his nose. "Let's take a vote, okay?" he said. "A show of paws. How many think Spikelle should have taken that last shot?"

Spikelle raised her paw. She raised it high. To her surprise, no other paws went into the air. Not a one.

Spikelle felt her spines go cold. Then they went mushy. Then they went prickly. They went prickly and hot.

"That's crazy," she said. "You guys are nuts."

Spikelle stood. She stomped out of the locker room. Two words echoed in her mind . . .

Ball hog . . . Ball hog . . . Ball hog.

CHAPTER 3

WILD SPINES

Spikelle felt badly after the game. On her way home, she stopped at Healy's Pond.

A wooden bench sat near the water. It was her favorite place to think.

What were her teammates talking about? Why were they complaining? The Hedgehogs usually won, and Spikelle was usually the main reason. Didn't they like to win? Were they simply upset she had missed the last shot? Did they blame her for losing the game?

Some ducks swam by. They were huddled together like a happy little team. Spikelle sighed. She wondered what her teammates were saying about her at that very moment.

Spikelle and Maddy had been friends since they were little. Most of the time, Spikelle practiced alone. But she sometimes practiced with Maddy, too. Or the others. Maybe Spikelle should have just passed it to Maddy. Maybe Maddy should have taken the last shot. Spikelle tried to imagine that.

It was very hard for Spikelle to imagine Maddy taking the last shot. In Spikelle's imagination, Spikelle was always the star. Spikelle was the one who took the last shot. And in Spikelle's imagination, her shot always went in.

But in the game, Spikelle's final shot had missed the hoop by a mile.

Did that mean her imagination was wrong? Were her teammates right? *Was* she a ball hog?

Spikelle shook her head. She rubbed her spines. That's when she felt something strange. Her headband was missing. Now the spines on her head were spiking up everywhere.

Spikelle was named for these wild spines. She usually held them in place — mostly, anyway — with her lucky headband while playing on the court. She had gotten the headband as a present from her grandfather. He was quite the player in the old days. He had wild, spiky spines, too.

But now that lucky headband was gone.

Usually after a game, Spikelle liked to get right back on the court. She liked to practice moves or shots that hadn't worked in the game.

But now all the extra practice felt pointless.

Maybe, she thought, *I'll never shoot again.*

CHAPTER FOUR

WILD PASSES

Spikelle showed up early for practice. She wanted to check the locker room for her missing headband. Maddy had not yet arrived. Neither had any of the other hedgehogs.

Spikelle checked her locker for the headband. She checked other lockers. She checked her sports bag. She checked everywhere. It wasn't there.

She went out into the gym. She dribbled in circles — left paw and right. She didn't shoot. Coach Furball and her teammates arrived. They appeared on the court, one by one.

"Anybody seen my headband?" Spikelle said.

Everyone shook their heads no.

"Well, it's missing," she said. "It's my good luck charm, you know." She said all of this in an angry way. She hadn't meant to, but she had. She realized that she had been wondering the whole time if someone stole it.

No one said anything. To Spikelle, it seemed that no one even cared.

Coach Furball blew his whistle. "Layups. Let's go."

The Hedgehogs formed lines. They took turns dribbling hard to the hoop and taking close shots. All except Spikelle, that is. She dribbled fast, but when it came time to shoot the ball, she just passed it to the next hedgehog in line.

After two or three times, Coach spoke up. "What are you doing, Spikelle?"

"Passing," said Spikelle.

During the team scrimmage, Spikelle played hard, as usual. She just did not shoot. Which was unusual. Very unusual.

She did throw a lot of passes. She threw bounce passes. She threw chest passes. She threw behind-the-back passes. She threw between-the-legs passes. She threw no-look passes, underpaw passes, and all sorts of passes with tricky spin. And Spikelle threw all of these passes HARD.

Her teammates wanted her to pass more, eh?

How about that? she thought, throwing a wicked one-paw pass.

How about that!

How about that!!!

After a third pass of Spikelle's hit Roxy Roller in the forehead, Roxy lost her cool.

"What's up with you, Spikelle?" Roxy said.

Spikelle wiped her wild spines out of her eyes. She looked a little scary. "I thought you wanted more passes," said Spikelle.

"You're just being mean," said Roxy.

Nearby, Maddy began to laugh.

It made Spikelle mad. "What are you laughing at?" said Spikelle.

Maddy covered her mouth with her paws. Then she pointed at Spikelle's head.

"What's so funny?" hollered Spikelle.

Maddy said, "Your spines are as wild as your passes."

"That's because you stole my headband, Maddy!" Spikelle yelled.

"I did not!" shouted Maddy.

Coach Furball blew his whistle. "Easy, now!" said Coach. "Easy."

Spikelle ran to the locker room. She flung open Maddy's locker and began to rummage through it. She threw all of Maddy's stuff onto the floor.

Maddy came in. "What are you doing?" she said. "Stay out of my locker!"

"I'm looking for my headband!" said Spikelle.

"Why don't you just get another one?" said Maddy.

"My grandfather gave me that headband!" Spikelle said. She turned on Maddy. Her spines stuck out angry and sharp. "Where did you put my lucky headband?" she growled.

"I . . . didn't . . . take it," said Maddy. She balled up. Her spines stuck out, too.

The Hedgehogs' two star guards stepped toward each other. They were ready to tangle. Coach Furball showed up just in time to stop the fight.

CHAPTER 5

TAKING ON THE SKINKS

The Hedgehogs were traveling to play the Skinks. The team bus rumbled down the road.

Spikelle sat in a seat up near the front of the bus. She watched out the window as trees whizzed by. One seat in front of her sat Coach Furball. He was curled up and napping. Her teammates were having a good old time in the back of the bus. Giggling, snorting, and thumping music filled the air.

Spikelle ran a paw through her spines. She gathered up a few wild ones and sighed to herself. She put on her new headband, a plain white one. It didn't feel so lucky.

Coach Furball began to stir and whimper in his sleep.

Spikelle put a paw on Coach's shoulder. She said, "It's okay, Coach."

Coach opened his eyes. He looked confused.

"It's me, Spikelle," said Spikelle. "We're on the bus. Were you dreaming?"

Coach sniffed the air. He looked around. He grunted and cleared his throat. "Nightmare," he said. "I dreamed we were playing the Skinks."

"We *are* playing the Skinks," said Spikelle. "Like, in about an hour."

"It was storming in the gym," said Coach. "It was very dark. Rain and thunder and lightning came from the roof. The Skinks had a hundred players on the court. They slithered this way and that. The winners were going to eat the losers."

"Whoa," said Spikelle. "Were we winning?"

"We were losing," said Coach. "You would only pass but not shoot."

Spikelle patted Coach on the shoulder. "It was just a dream," she said.

Coach Furball frowned. "It felt pretty real to me," he said.

Maddy came up. "Well, that dream won't come true because I found this," she said. She held out a red headband with white stars on it.

Spikelle's lucky headband.

"It was by the water's edge at Healy's Pond," said Maddy.

Spikelle didn't know what to say. Was Maddy telling the truth? Did she find it at the pond, or did she steal it? Spikelle looked closely at Maddy. It was difficult to read Maddy's face.

Spikelle took the headband and said, "Thanks."

"Does this mean you two will get along?" asked Coach.

Maddy walked to the back of the bus, back to the other hedgehogs. Soon the bus stopped. All the players grabbed their bags and filed out of the bus.

Spikelle put her headband on. It fit just right. She knew it was just a headband. But still. It made her feel like herself again.

* * *

Inside the gym the Hedgehog and Skink fans were going crazy. The two teams were huddled by their benches for a timeout.

The scoreboard's numbers told the story. Skinks 59, Hedgehogs 58. Five seconds left.

Hedgehog fans waved foam paws and sang out, "**LET'S GO HEDGIES!**" *Clap clap. Clap clap clap.*

Skink fans flicked their tails and clapped their clammy hands. They shouted, "Go big **GREEN!** Go big **GREEN!**"

The Skinks were smart players. They would keep low when they had the ball. Sometimes they would dribble or pass the ball with their tails. They were slippery on offense. They were even slicker on defense.

Spikelle and Maddy had kept the Hedgehogs in the contest. They had played the games of their lives. From the opening tip, they worked together like the old friends they were.

Spikelle passed to Maddy. Maddy passed back to Spikelle. Maddy and Spikelle passed to their teammates. Their teammates passed back.

Suddenly, everyone had wide open shots. When Spikelle and Maddy were open, they didn't miss, even if their teammates sometimes did.

The problem was, the Hedgehogs were tired. The Skinks seemed to never slow down.

Inside the Hedgehogs huddle, Coach Furball looked at his team. He was very shaky.

"Well," said Maddy. "What's the play?"

Coach Furball looked around. "Now where did my clipboard marker go?" he said.

Coach Furball turned right. He turned left. He spun in a circle three times. When he stopped, his eyes were crossed. Sweat flew from the fur on his forehead.

One of the players pointed to Coach's feet, where his marker lay. A couple of the Hedgehog players rolled their eyes.

Coach laughed. He was embarrassed. He picked the clipboard up but didn't say anything.

Spikelle spoke up. "I've got a plan," she said. "Do you mind if I speak, Coach?"

Coach mopped his forehead with a towel. He slicked back his fur. "Go ahead, Spikelle," he said.

"Okay," said Spikelle. "I'll pass it in. Maddy, you take the last shot."

Many of the Hedgehogs could not believe their ears.

"Okay," said Maddy. "But there may be time for a pick and roll."

"That's true," said Spikelle. "If they guard you tight, I'll pick for you."

"Got it," said Maddy. "Everybody else . . . stay ready! If I can't shoot, I may pass."

Coach Furball smiled. "Good plan. Put your paws together now."

The Hedgehogs put their paws together.

"One, two, three . . ." Coach Furball said.

"**HOGS!**" said the team.

The players took their places.

The referee held the ball out for Spikelle. Spikelle smiled at the referee and took it. She slapped the ball.

The Hedgehogs players went into motion.

Maddy broke free, and Spikelle passed the ball to her.

The clock began to move. Five . . . four . . .

Spikelle saw that Maddy was double-teamed. She set a pick. Maddy dribbled free, and Spikelle rolled toward the basket.

Three . . . two . . .

Maddy threw Spikelle the perfect bounce pass. Spikelle caught it and prepared to shoot.

But a smarty Skink jumped up for the block. Out of the corner of Spikelle's eye, she saw Roxy Roller right under the hoop. She fired a pass . . .

One . . .

Roxy caught the hard pass and flipped up a shot.

The buzzer **BLARED**.

Roxy's shot rolled around the rim once . . . and then twice . . . and went in the hoop.

The crowd went nuts. Hedgehog fans danced and hugged. Skink fans groaned and cried.

The Hedgehog players ran around the court.

"Great shot!" said Spikelle to Roxy.

"Great pass!" said Roxy.

Maddy ran up, smiling. "Great teamwork!" she shouted.

Spikelle threw her headband into the air. She and her teammates jumped up and down in a giant, happy, spiky ball.

ABOUT THE AUTHOR

Born on the range in Montana and raised partly by wolves (just kidding, unless you count his three big brothers), Hoss Masterson is no stranger to living the life wild. By trade, he's been a hired farmhand, a sportswriter, a teacher, and a musician (bass guitar and harmonica). He enjoys old Westerns, birdwatching, cropchecking, and a good yarn.

ABOUT THE ILLUSTRATOR

International award-winning illustrator Josh Alves loves creating art and visiting schools to encourage creativity. He lives in Maine with his incredible wife and their four clever kids. Learn more about him at www.joshalves.com.

GLOSSARY

clipboard (KLIP-bohrd) – a small board a coach uses to draw up plays

huddle (HUD-uhl) – a closely gathered group of players who listen to a coach or player for instructions

inbound (IN-bownd) – to pass the ball in from out of bounds

jump shot (JUMP shot) – a shot where a player jumps up before shooting

layup (LAY-up) – a close-up shot taken while running toward the basket

referee (reh-fuh-REE) – a judge who makes sure players follow the rules

skink (SKINK) – a small lizard with a long body

spines (SPINES) – sharp, pointed parts on an animal like long, stiff hairs

TALK ABOUT IT!

1. Why did Spikelle not want to pass? Should anyone get to take the last shot?

2. Why didn't Spikelle shoot during practice after being called a ball hog?

3. Why were the Hedgehogs better when they started playing as a team?

WRITE ABOUT IT!

1. Make a list of reasons Spikelle gave for thinking she deserved to take the last shot.

2. Write a story about Spikelle's grandpa when he was a young hedgehog.

3. Write a hedgehog poem using hedgehog words like spines, paw, and roll.

HEDGEHOG FACTS

- feature 15 species, including some from Europe, Asia, and Africa

- are awake at night more often than day

- like to be by themselves most the time

- can live up to five years

- have superb senses of smell and hearing, but poor eyesight

- possess about 5,000 spines that re-grow when they fall out after a year's time

- protect themselves by rolling into a ball and showing their spiky coat

THE FUN DOESN'T STOP HERE!

DISCOVER MORE AT WWW.CAPSTONEKIDS.COM

VIDEOS & CONTESTS · GAMES & PUZZLES
FRIENDS & FAVORITES · AUTHORS & ILLUSTRATORS

Find cool websites and more books like this
one at www.facthound.com. Just type in the
book ID, and you're ready to go!
Book ID: 9781496543080